# LITTLE LOKSI

*Little Loksi*


ISBN: 978-1-935684-72-5

Book Design: Corey Fetters

White Dog Press
c/o Chickasaw Press
PO Box 1548
Ada, Oklahoma 74821

chickasawpress.com

# LITTLE LOKSI

Chokma!
May you use your talents to help others along your journey!
Chipisala'cho
Trey Hays
11/9/19

By Trey Hays • Illustrated By Eli Corbin

Dedicated to the Oklahoma Arts Institute, for supporting fine arts in schools for more than forty years, and to my son Jax, for teaching me that everything on this planet has a purpose, even the stink of a skunk.

- Trey Hays

One afternoon the Loksi family went for a walk. They walked along a rough and rocky place.

They went up and down the hills and valleys, over the logs and rocks, and under the brush and bushes.

They went through dry creek beds and creek beds with trickles of water bubbling through the rocks.

They walked past
a pond with waves
splashing against the
shore. Little Loksi was
hit by an extra big
wave, and suddenly he
was turned over onto
his back! Oh no!

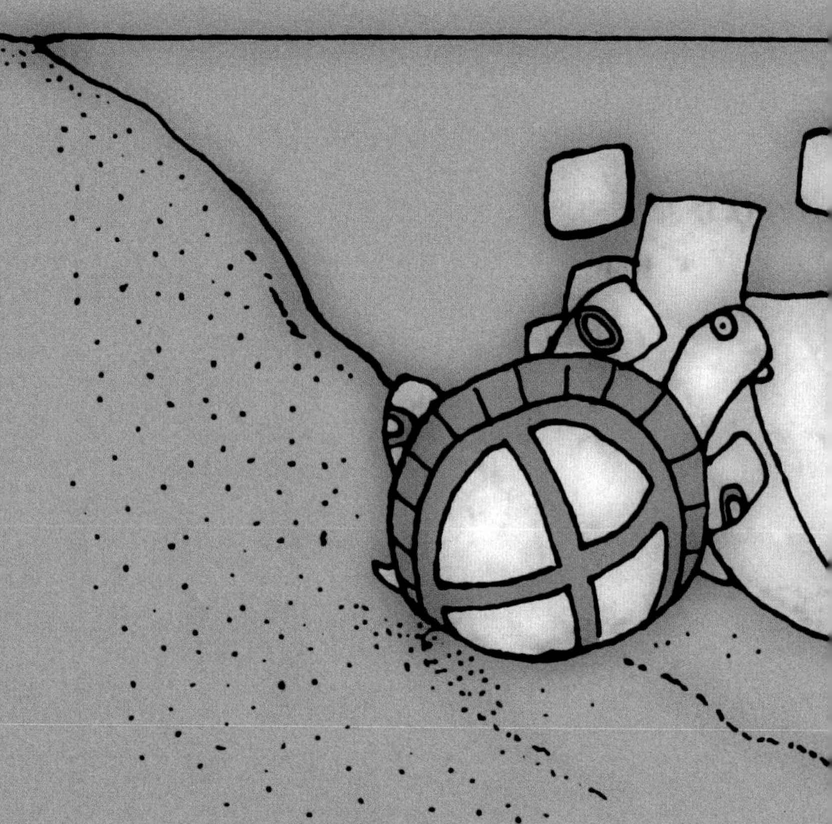

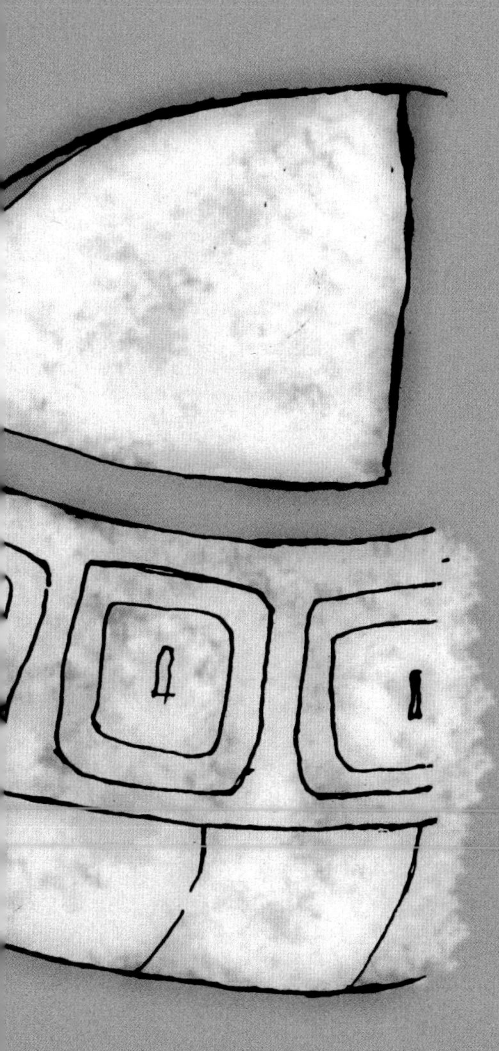

The other turtles gathered around him and tried to turn him over. Daddy Loksi put his head under Little Loksi's shell and pushed with all his might. He could not turn him over!

The first animal to come
waddling by was Fochush.
He saw the trouble Little
Loksi was having and said,
"Maybe I can turn him over
with my long bill."

So Fochush
wedged his bill
under Little
Loksi's shell
and pushed, but
the turtle just
slipped right off.
Fochush could
not do it!

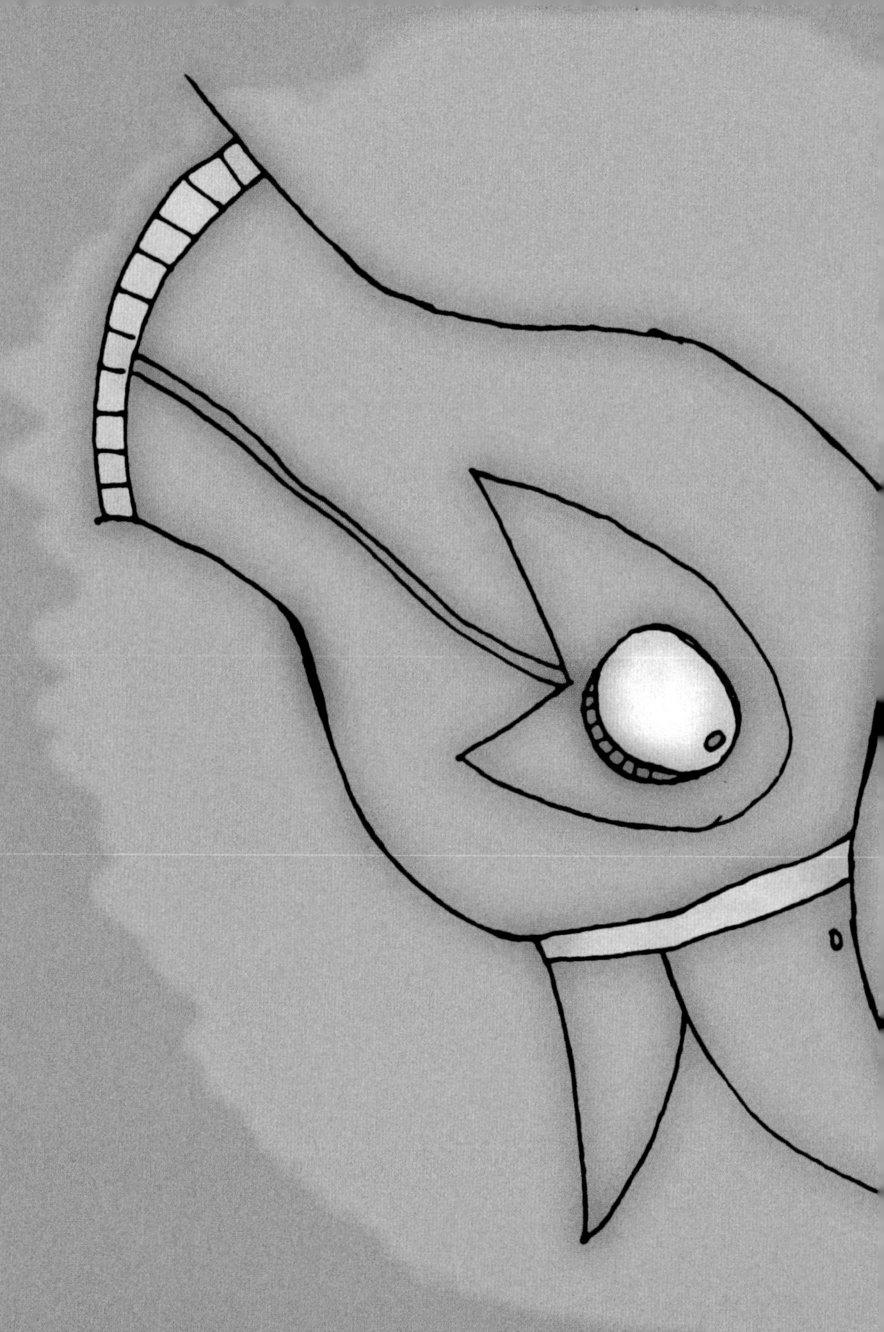

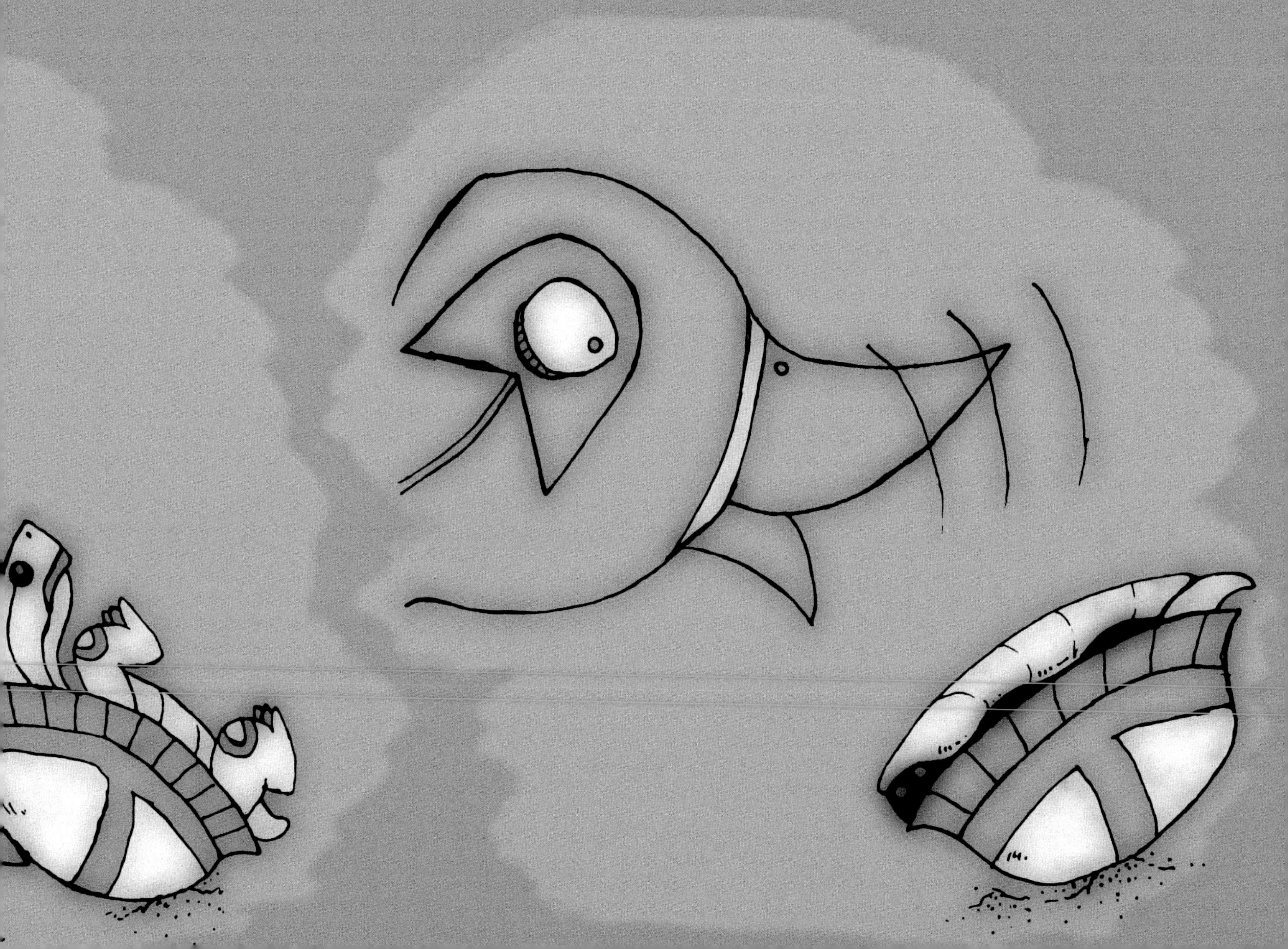

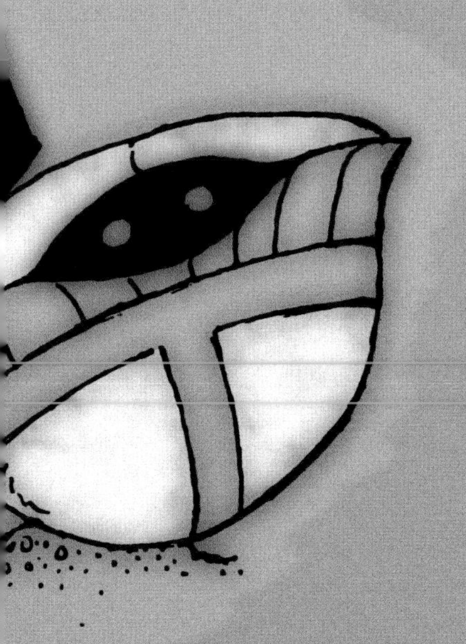

Soba was galloping through the woods and barely managed to jump over Little Loksi. "Hika! I'm glad I missed you little fella," exclaimed Soba. He used his hoof to gently paw Little Loksi.

**Little Loksi rocked back and forth, but he couldn't wobble enough to turn over.**

Next to come hopping by was Chukfi. He playfully said, "Hey, little buddy, it appears you have a hurdle to overcome there."

Chukfi wasn't sure how he could help Little Loksi turn over. He told him the story about how Little Loksi's grandfather had beat Chukfi's grandfather in a race long ago.

The race taught them all you should never stop trying and everyone has something that makes him or her special. Chukfi couldn't turn Little Loksi over, but he could help him to feel better. After all, Little Loksi was still alive and had friends and family gathered around to keep him company.

Night fell. The moon came out, and all sorts of sounds echoed in the woods. Chukfi told the animals stories about the moon and stars. Little Loksi had never seen the sky in such majestic beauty before.

Nashoba had been watching and listening from a distance and was inspired by Chukfi's stories. Nashoba howled as Chukfi spoke about the moon. Nashoba said in his husky voice, "I will go out and search for someone who can help Little Loksi."

Nashoba ran through the woods until he found the tree where Osi kept her perch. He told her the problem. She said, "I am sorry Nashoba. I cannot fly at night, but I will come to help as soon as I see daylight."

Nashoba continued his search for someone who could help Little Loksi.

Surely there was someone who had the talent they needed.

**Nashoba moved through the woods and suddenly his eyes began to water. He recognized Koni's powerful smell.**

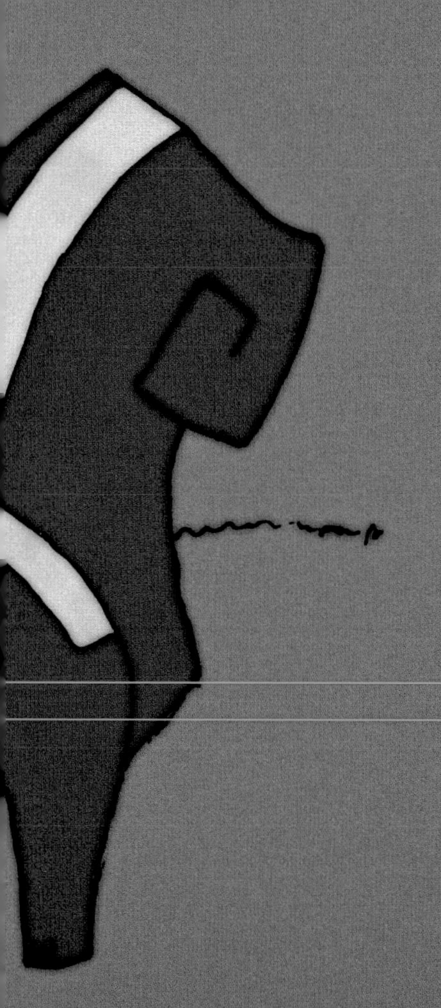

Nashoba choked out a question, "Koni, would you guard a friend with your powerful smell?" Koni agreed to go help Little Loksi by keeping away scoundrels who might see him as dinner.

Nashoba met Haknip Hishi' Haloppa' next. Haknip Hishi' Haloppa' was usually calm and kept to himself, but when he got scared his sharp quills protected him from friend and foe alike.

Nashoba asked Haknip Hishi' Haloppa' to be a part of the crowd of critters helping Little Loksi. He could challenge anyone sneaking past Koni's powerful smell.

Nashoba continued searching for the perfect animal to help Little Loksi. Suddenly, he found himself caught in a sticky spider web, which gave him an idea!

The critter who could turn Little Loksi back over was Cholhkun. Her webs were really strong. The silk threads from Cholhkun could be weaved around Little Loksi's legs.

Nashoba spoke very softly,
"Cholhkun, I have been searching
for a friend to help Little Loksi.
Your web could be the secret to
turning him back over. Could
you please climb on my back?"
Cholhkun agreed, and they made
the long journey back.

When they arrived, all of the animals were asleep. The night was almost over and dawn was breaking. Cholhkun got right to work.

She quickly spun her web around two of Little Loksi's legs. As she spun, the web grew stronger and stronger.

Just as the sun came over the mountain, Cholhkun finished spinning her web between Little Loksi's legs. Then, Osi swooped down, caught the web, and pulled it as she flew. Little Loksi was safely back on his feet!

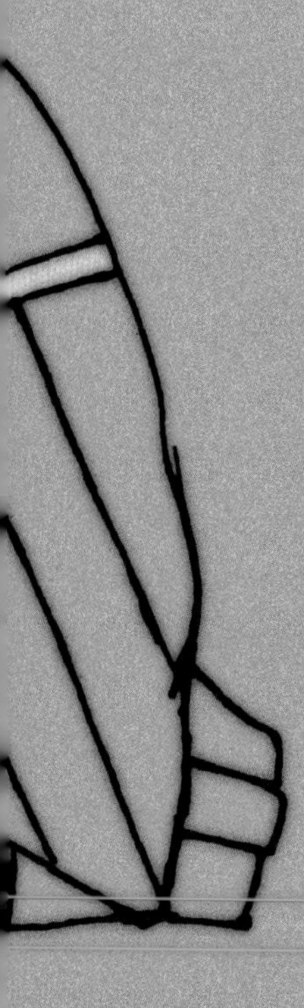

Little Loksi and his family
were thankful for all the
animals who used their unique
skills and talents to help him.

As they all gathered around, Nashoba reminded them how important each of them and their special talents were in the great cycle of life.

**Nashoba said, "Some talents keep us safe from danger. Some talents help us achieve goals and overcome struggles. When we use our talents to help each other, everyone is better for it."**

Everybody cheered and did an animal song and dance, for music is a talent everyone has. Soba trotted in rhythm. The turtles moved their heads side to side and stomped slowly. The birds sang, Fochush waddled and quacked, and Chukfi hippity-hopped.

At the end of the celebration Cholhkun made a web, and everyone held on and danced in a circle. For weaving webs was her talent, and everyone was better for it.

· THE END ·

**The Chickasaw language is an important part of our culture. It's part of what makes us uniquely Chickasaw. This glossary will help you identify and pronounce the animals within the story in Chickasaw!**

| English | Chickasaw | Pronunciation |
| --- | --- | --- |
| duck | fochush | foh-choosh |
| eagle | *o*si | ohn-se |
| horse | soba | soh-bah |
| porcupine | haknip hishi' haloppa' | hak-nip hi-shi ha-lop-pa |
| rabbit | chukfi | chook-fe |
| skunk | koni | koh-ne |
| spider | cholhkun | cholh-kun |
| turtle | loksi | lohk-se |
| whoa | hika | he-kah |
| wolf | nashoba | nah-shoh-bah |

# LITTLE LOKSI